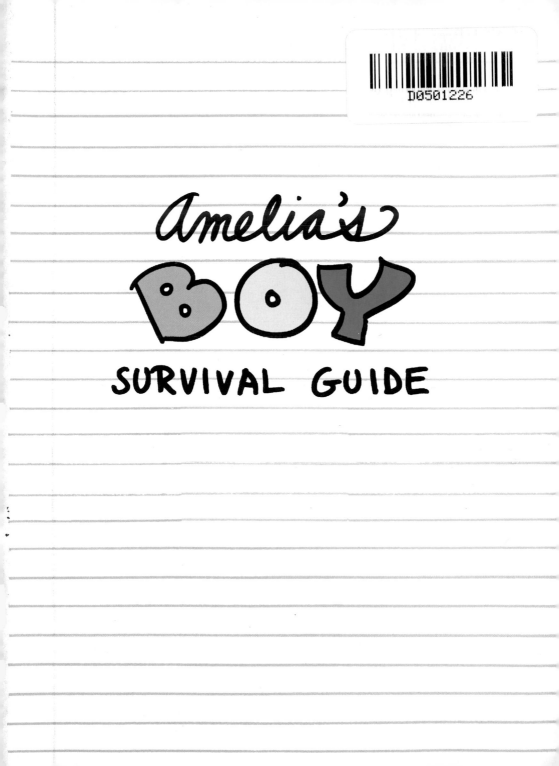

Amelia's BOY SURVIVAL GUIDE

Amelia's BOY SURVIVAL GUIDE

by Marissa Moss
(and totally confused Amelia)

Simon & Schuster Books for Young Readers

New York   London   Toronto   Sydney   New Delhi

SIMON & SCHUSTER BOOKS FOR YOUNG READERS
An imprint of Simon & Schuster Children's Publishing Division

1230 Avenue of the Americas, New York, New York, 10020

For information about special discounts for bulk purchases, please
contact Simon & Schuster Special Sales at 1-866-506-1949 or
business@simonandschuster.com.

The Simon & Schuster Speakers Bureau can bring authors to your
live event. For more information, contact the Simon & Schuster
Speakers Bureau at 1-866-248-3049 or visit our website at
www.simonspeakers.com.

Also available in a SIMON & SCHUSTER BOOKS FOR YOUNG READERS hardcover edition

A Paula Wiseman Book
Book design by Amelia
(with help from Tom Daly)

No boys
were harmed
in the making
of this book-
or girls, either! →

The text for this book is hand-lettered.
Manufactured in China
1214 SCP
2   4   6   8   10   9   7   5   3   1

First SIMON & SCHUSTER BOOKS FOR YOUNG READERS
paperback edition March 2015

Library of Congress Control Number: 2011278418

ISBN 978-1-4424-4084-5 (hc)
ISBN 978-1-4424-4085-2 (pbk)
ISBN 978-1-4424-4086-9 (eBook)

This book is dedicated
to my three boys —
Simon, Elias, and Asa.

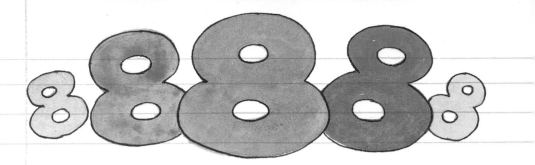

Don't 8's look like such friendly, happy numbers? All jolly and ho, ho, ho-like? Maybe they're not lucky numbers, like 7's and 4's, but they're a super special number to me. Especially today.

Magic 8 ball →

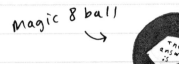

The answer is yes!

Magic Number 8! ←

Because that magic day has finally come, the best day of ALL the days I've gone to school:

MY FIRST DAY AS AN 8TH GRADER!

Sure, starting kindergarten was fun and exciting, and 5th grade was great because I was at the top of the heap of elementary school.

Welcome, Kindergartners!!

I remember how excited I was to see a cute little cubby with my name on it for me to put my lunch in. Getting a locker was nowhere near as fun.

But 8th grade, that's REALLY special, because now I'm not just at the top of the heap — I'm at the top of the MIDDLE SCHOOL heap. That's a HUGE deal!

I want to savor every second because part of what makes 8th grade so great is what comes next.

9th grade.

Meaning high school.

That's something I'm not eager for at all. If 6th grade was scary, 9th is terrifying! And does it mean something that they're basically the same number upside-down and right-side-up?

Does that mean that 9th grade is like 6th, only turned around?—which would be good, I guess. Or does it mean they're mirror images of each other, both awful?

At least I don't have to think about that yet. For now I can bask in my superior 8th gradeness.

And admire the round symmetry of 8. →

It's not like any number except itself, and maybe double zero, like a secret agent.

What makes this year even better is that my best friend, Carly, has almost all the same classes as me. At the same time, with the same teacher!! That's rarer than finding money on the street or winning the school drawing for class pizza day. But this year, this marvelous 8th-grade year, it's like we won the lottery!

We have first and second periods together, English and Social Studies with Mr. Hoyle.

↑

I've heard that Mr. Hoyle is a good teacher, tough but fair and, most important, interesting! He looks kind of like a toad and sounds a bit croaky, but so long as he isn't boring, that's fine with me.

Third period we have math with Mrs. Darcey.

Some kids like her, some kids hate her, so I'm not sure what to expect. →

All I can say is that she likes to wear shirts with big, floppy bows in front, like she's a package being gift-wrapped. ← wrapped.

↑ And she draws her eyebrows on with pencil so she looks perpetually surprised.

Though not as bad as Ms. Jareau, the horrible substitute French teacher from last year. ↓

Eyebrows should be here, but she shaved them off.

and drew new ones _way_ up here that looked like circumflex marks. Why?

↑ Is she punctuating her face?

French with Mr. Le Poivre (not the substitute) is fourth period, another class Carly and I have together.

We had Mr. LePoivre → last year and the year before.

He gives lots of homework, but class will ← be fun, especially with Carly there!

The last class we share is Science with Ms. Singh.

She's the oldest teacher I've ever had, like grandmother age. I bet → she remembers black and white television.

She wears thick shoes and flower print dresses that look like they're about a ← century old. Maybe they are.

At the end of the day are the only two classes we have apart. Carly has P.E., then Art. I have Art, then P.E. I hate having P.E. as the last class of all because you're already hot and tired and you just get MORE hot and tired. Carly says it's a good last class because by then your brain is soggy and worn out, and thinking is something you don't need to do at all in P.E. She has a point there.

You don't usually see your brain doing push-ups.
↓

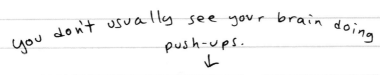

Or playing volleyball.
↓

Or baseball.
↓

I'm too smart for that.

WHAP!

Wake me when the game is over.

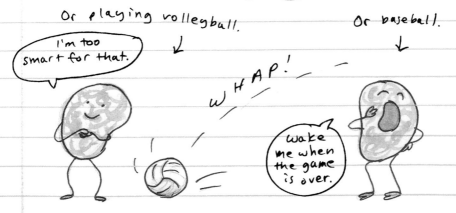

But I think Art is the best class to have last because it's like dessert, the delicious cherry on top of the day, so you have a good taste in your mouth when you head home.

Ms. Oates — I mean "Star" — would love that description. She thinks art can save the world.

↓

we'll tap into your creative energy.

And free the magic for all to see!

↑

I've taken Art from her in 6th grade, 7th grade, and now 8th. She's a good teacher, and I like her a lot. But I still can't call her Star to her face the way she wants us to. I'm just not artistic enough for that.

Anyway, the day started out shiny and bright like a new quarter with Carly and me walking to class together.

Carly ↓

me ↙

↑

Two proud 8th graders, walking with our heads held high, our backpacks still light since we hadn't gotten any heavy textbooks yet. It was the first time I started a new school year and didn't worry about looking like a dork.

It's funny how the lowly 6th and 7th graders don't exist anymore once you're an 8th grader. They're like a sea of fog way beneath you.

When they talk, it's like the chatter of birds chirping or squirrels chittering, but no words.

cheee cheee cheee *

I remember when I started 6th grade, how scary the 8th graders seemed. Now I'm the scary one!

* translation: "Which girls' bathroom is safe to use?"

"Aren't they so cute and little?" Carly asked.

"Who cares about them?" I said. "Aren't we big and   powerful?"

I felt like for once ↑ in my life, I had real muscles — 8th grade muscles!

"Just don't let it go to your head or anything."

"Come on, Carly! I want to enjoy this while I can. How many times do I get to have this feeling?"

She had to admit I had a point. And I was right to relish my 8th grade status because once class started, reality did, too.

Meaning sure we're big deal 8th graders, but we still have homework, tests, boring lectures, and the usual lists of rules.

No eating in class.
No gum chewing.
No talking out of turn.
No alien abductions.
No flights of fancy.
No getting bright ideas.
No clichés at all.
No fun — of course.

NO!

But here's the BIGGEST news about 8th grade — the boys are WAY cuter than 7th graders. Which is ~~weird~~ ~~weird~~ ~~weird~~ ~~weird~~ WEIRD! Most of them are the exact same boys from last year, but something happened to them over the summer. They're taller, have actual muscles, and their voices are deeper.

Even as an 8th grader, I can't spell this! Is there hope I'll finally get it right in 9th grade?

Some guys who were too smelly to go near before, actually look okay now. And some of the ones who were okay as 7th graders are _cute_ as 8th graders.

Like Gerald Lammercy. He sits in front of me in first period, English/Social Studies, so I can study his ears and shoulders.

Gerald from the back— even his ears are adorable.

Gerald from the front. Most boys don't have much in the way of eyelashes, but he sure does!

I wrote Carly a note.

Do you think Gerald is cute?

I started to pass it to her when

DISASTER!

tightly folded note → ← dropped on the floor!

Gerald picked up the note, and I thought my heart would stop. What if he READ it?! I was doomed!

This is what total panic looks like. →

The seconds ticked by like hours. ↙

Then a miracle happened — Gerald passed the note to Carly for me WITHOUT opening it. He's not only cute, he's totally WONDERFUL!!!

I smiled at him to show him how grateful I was. ↘

He has no idea HOW grateful. And relieved! ↙

I watched Carly unfold the note in her lap and read it. She looked at me and winked. She could tell how great Gerald is just by his gentlemanly note-passing.

That's another thing Carly does perfectly — winking. →

Which is something I really admire because a wink is like no other gesture.

↑
It's like a secret smile, a whisper with your face. And it's something I can't do at all.

I look all squinchy whenever → I try.

I'm a total wink failure!

Suddenly it hit me — if I can't wink, if I'm such a loser, what will Gerald think of me? Does <u>he</u> think I'<u>m</u> cute? Or at least not ugly? Does he like me? "Like" like me? Is he being nice to me or just polite?

Is there something I can do, some way I can act so he will like me? Could I help him pass his own notes? Is he the note-passing type? How can I make him notice me?

Have I changed a lot over the summer, too? Am I the kind of girl a boy could like?

I have my doubts.

I've never been one of the cute, popular girls. Why should that change just because I'm in 8th grade? The thing is, I didn't care about being cool before. Well, I did care, but I was fine with having a few good friends and not worrying about the rest.

Does liking a boy mean I need to worry more? It feels like it! UGH!! I can't believe I'm thinking this way. If I'm not careful, I'll turn into Cleo!

Cleo
↓

my older sister is in 10th grade and totally boy crazy.
They're all she talks about —
↙ really!

Despite how obnoxious she is, Cleo must be doing something right because she always has a boyfriend. Are guys blind in some ways that they don't care about all her gross habits?

She chews with her mouth open.

She snorts when she laughs.

She picks her nose with her pinky finger.

She sings way off-key, LOUDLY!

With Cleo as an example, I really have no idea how to make a guy like me. Being like her can't work — I refuse to believe it!

At lunch Carly said I had it bad.

I didn't know what she was talking about. What "it"? What "bad"?

"The moonies for Gerald," she explained.

I still didn't get it.

"You're mooning over him, like a sick cow. You've got a crush, girl!"

"I do not!" I lied. Carly's my best friend. Why can't I admit to her that I like a boy? I don't know, but I just can't.

But Carly wouldn't give up. "Why did you ask if I think he's cute? C'mon, Amelia, I can tell heart-racing, cheeks-burning, stomach-flipping crushes when I see them."

I was mortified! Am I that obvious?

If Carly can tell, does that mean Gerald can? How could I ever face him again?

My sandwich felt like a heavy wad of clay in my stomach. And there was no hiding how red my cheeks were. I could feel them flaming like neon signs.

"I'm just excited about being an 8th grader," I mumbled. "That's all."

It sounded lame, even to me. Carly certainly wasn't buying it. She gave me that look she has, the one where she sees right through me to the core.

I swear she has laser eyes something. ↙

C'mon, Carly, I thought, just let it go. For once! Really, it's impossible to keep secrets from that girl! But I wasn't ready to talk about Gerald, at least not yet. It was still too confusing to me. I wasn't sure if I liked him or not. I just knew I wanted him to like me.

"Okay, have it your way." Carly shrugged. "We'll talk about something else. Like the Back to School dance next Friday. Are you going? With Gerald maybe?"

"Carly! You said we'd change the subject!"
"We did. We're talking about the dance."
"And about Gerald." I shoved the rest
of my lunch into the crumpled bag. No
way I could eat another bite. "I'm not
going to any stupid dance. I always end
up standing around, looking like a
total doofus, while boys ask _you_ to
dance. Way to ruin the start of my perfect
8th grade year!"
"This year could be different."
Could it really?

No matter
how hard I
try, I'm
invisible
at dances. →

I've put on
make up,
borrowed
clothes from
Carly -
nothing
works! ←

MIDDLE SCHOOL DANCES

What you want to have happen:

① A boy — not a gross one — will ask you to dance.

May I have the honor?

② He'll tell you you're pretty.

You look really nice tonight.

③ People will see you dancing with him and won't think you're a loser anymore.

④ Another boy will ask you to dance. And then another!

Let's dance!

MIDDLE SCHOOL DANCES

What actually does happen:

① Someone will spill a drink on someone else.

Hey!

Oops!

Sorry!

② A toilet will get clogged
and overflow.

YIKES!

③ A teacher will tell a lame joke.

Have you heard the one about the potato and the carrot?

④ Palms will get sweaty, armpits will get
itchy, every pimple will look
three times bigger than usual.

Help!

⑤ A song everyone hates
will be played and booed at.

BOO!   *HISS!*   *UGH!*

So what's so fun about a school dance? Seems like a form of torture to me. Unless, of course, Gerald asks me to go. Then it would be a lot of fun!

Carly doesn't have to worry about these things. Boys always ask her to dance. It's only the first day of school, and I bet six guys already have crushes on her, By tomorrow, there'll be a dozen.

I stared at my best friend slurping her juice. What makes her so cool? I've tried to be more Carly-ish, but I never get it right. I'm stuck with being me, no matter what I do. If I was cool, I'd never:

Have a bad hair day →

Get humongous pimples. →

Have embarrassing food stains on my clothes.

Take goony school pictures. →

Get food stuck between my teeth.

Fart in public. ↓

POOT!

Step in dog poop.

The bell rang and it was time to go to Science, the last class I have with Carly. Guess who happens to be in the same class?

Gerald!

Maybe it's some kind of sign from the universe that he'll like me. After all, now he has twice the time to get to know me. Though that could be a bad thing since he also has twice the number of chances to notice annoying things about me (like on the previous page).

Carly poked me with her elbow. "Gerald's following you," she whispered. "Must mean he likes you."

At least she kept her voice low! She could have used a fake, dramatic, meant-to-be-overheard whisper. I was relieved she actually whispered. Still, I could feel my cheeks flame.

bright pink cheeks →

Stop it!

The dotted line means I whispered, too - really whispered. I wanted to be invisible!

Carly looked surprised, hurt even. "Hey, I'm your friend, remember? I didn't mean to bug you."

She was right. I totally overreacted. I almost made the number one friendship mistake — letting a boy come between you. But there wasn't time to apologize, because Ms. Singh was assigning us to our seats. I hate it when teachers do that, because chances are, you'll sit next to someone you don't like. Teachers never let you sit with friends. It's like a code of honor with them.

Just as I thought, Carly was put in the front row while I was way in the back. Which would be miserable except guess who sat next to me? Gerald!

↑
Gerald, with his beautiful eyes and gentle smile and handsome forehead. Can a forehead be handsome?

↑
Me, sneaking glances at him, totally discreetly, you'd never notice.

Since we were behind Carly, she couldn't see what we were doing. Not that we did anything. But if we became friends and started passing notes, she'd never know (unless I told her). This really IS a magical year!

Not that Gerald was particularly friendly. Not yet anyway. I was supposed to listen to Ms. Singh explain the class rules, but mostly I watched Gerald. Here's what I learned:

1. Gerald is as bored by long lists of rules as me — we have that in common!

2. He doodles a lot. So do I!

3. His profile is even cuter than the back of his head. Since I can't see my own profile or the back of my head, I have no idea about either one. I only worry about the front of my face. Should I worry about side and back views, too?

doggy doodles
↘

Gerald drew a lot of pooches.
↙

I was memorizing the freckles on Gerald's cheek when the door opened and a student handed Ms. Singh a note. I write "a student" as if the person was just a nameless, average somebody that you might pass in the hall or have in the same class, but never actually talk to.

Except it wasn't. It was a very specific somebody, the person that made last year so horrible, the person from 7th grade science who turned out to be the nightmare partner of the year for our science fair project.

Sadie
↓

It's horrible how this girl haunts me! ↘

She calls me names, accuses me of being unethical, of stealing her ideas, of taking credit for her hard work. ↙

None of it is true! She makes me sound like a monster! ↑

And now she's in my science class again!
Even worse, Ms. Singh put her in the empty seat
next to me. So now I have Gerald on one side
(the good side), Sadie on the other (the dark
side).

Gerald   me   Sadie
↓   ↓   ↓

↑

·I can't look at Gerald too much or Sadie will
notice. Her, I don't want to see at all! At least
she's not trying to be friends with me anymore,
but has she given up being enemies? From
the way she glared at me, I guess not.

Maybe I could ask Gerald to switch places
and he could be next to Sadie instead. I'd
have to ask Ms. Singh first. I could say I'm
allergic to Sadie's shampoo and need to
move. Except what if Sadie starts flirting
with Gerald and then he likes her instead
of me?

Is that possible? Is Sadie the kind of girl boys like? The kind Gerald likes? How can I tell? There's no figuring out why boys like the girls they do — look at Cleo and all her boyfriends! Except when the girl is Carly and then it's obvious why every single boy in the world likes her.

So I'm back to sitting between Good and Bad. If Ms. Singh makes us partners for anything, I'll scream!

Carly knows the whole Sadie saga. When class was over, she hurried to rescue me from Sadie's evil eye.

C'mon, Amelia, let's go!

Um, yeah.

Carly said I should be grateful that Sadie's only in one class with me. So far. Who knows about P.E. and Art?

"Cheer up, Amelia! We're 8th graders now. Nothing can be that bad. Besides, even if you sit next to Sadie, you also sit next to your crush."

"He's not my crush!" I said. "And even if he was, that's ruined by sitting next to you-know-who."

Carly rolled her eyes. She didn't have to say a word, I could tell what she was thinking.

glass half full →

← glass half empty

↑

Carly is an optimist. She always sees the positive parts of something, the glass that's half full. Me, I'm not sure what I see. Sometimes the glass is half full, sometimes half empty. Sometimes it's all smudgy and needs washing.

It's like an optical illusion. →

Do you see a vase or two faces in profile? ←

Vase or faces?

One thing I'm always positive about is Art. That class is always fun. It was a relief to be back in that familiar, messy room.

Ms. Oates was pinning up a poster with big, inspiring letters.

There were several kids I knew from last year, but no Sadie. Phew! No Gerald, either, but that would really be expecting too much even if he does love to doodle dogs.

A couple of boys were kinda cute, but nowhere near Geraldness. I can't believe I wrote that! I'm rating boys' cuteness now! What am I turning into?

SCALE OF BOY

10 In-your-dreams fabulous with charming smile, deep rich voice, absolutely perfect!

9 Super-cute with big eyes, nice teeth, broad shoulders, perfect nose (a little big is okay — that shows character).

8 Handsome face and real muscles — a killer combination.

7 Better than okay — a nice face, good hair, and toned muscles.

6 Pretty good. Maybe not much muscle, but a great face.

If I was a better artist, I could draw cuteness better. As it is, these boys look a <u>lot</u> alike.

CUTENESS

Basically okay. If he asked you to dance, you'd say yes.

5

Acceptable. No major grossness like a boogery nose or slimy green teeth.

4

3

Dangerous territory. Steer clear of tangled hair and body odor. Does he sleep in a barn?

Not your type. Or anybody else's!

2

No way, no how, NOT EVER!

1

I know it's horribly superficial of me to rate boys by their looks, but this is my PRIVATE notebook, so no one will ever know.

Of course personality matters, too, but there are super-nice boys who just aren't on the possible boyfriend scale. They can be friends, but not boyfriends. There's no explaining that, it's just the way it is.

Not that I'm an expert, but I've had boys be perfectly good partners on group projects, I've liked them fine, but they didn't give me the stomach flutters that Gerald does.

It's all a mystery.

Kind of like art and creativity. You can't make them happen. They just do.

And you know good art when you see it. There are no rules, just a gut feeling.

To me, this isn't good art. ↓

It's a giant scribble. →

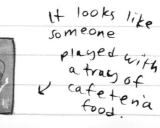

It looks like someone played with a tray of cafeteria food. ↙

I give Ms. Oates credit — she's the only teacher who didn't start class with a long list of rules, the same ones I've heard since kindergarten. We all know them, so why do teachers bother?

Rules for Good Behavior

If you do something good, you get a gold star →

☆ ☆ ☆ = ☺   ☺ ☺ ☺ = ☀

☀ ☀ ☀ = one class movie

Which would be a great reward except the movie is always a documentary on cardboard or the history of plumbing.

Rules for Bad Behavior

If you do something bad, you get a 🙁 ← frowny face

🙁 🙁 🙁 = ☁🌧

🌧 🌧 🌧 = one warning

3 warnings = 1 referral, 3 referrals = 1 detention where you watch a documentary on cardboard or the history of plumbing.

Ms. Oates started class by having us talk about why we chose to take Art. You'd think she'd know by now that she'd get answers like these:

I felt bad for her, so when it was my turn, I told the truth. I said I like Art because I love to draw and I feel more creative in Art than in any other class.

Somehow that made it okay to like Art, and the next kid said she chose Art because it's fun. A boy said he wanted to make better comics. Another boy loved painting. Then everyone was talking about favorite colors, about markers versus colored pencils, about watercolors versus acrylic paint. It was a real artists' discussion. Ms. Oates was so excited, she fluttered around like a giant butterfly.

It sounds like we're going to do some really cool stuff this year, like printmaking. Maybe it's a good thing Gerald's not in the class so I don't get distracted. And no Sadie so I won't be tormented.

Our first project is a self-portrait. That's one of Ms. Oates's favorite assignments. She thinks it's good for us to see how we've changed and grown.

Have I?

what's different about this face? Am I finally cute as an 8th grader? →

Last year my self-portrait was a black silhouette with a notebook attached to it, kind of like a portrait of my brain.

This year, I can't help wondering if I'm pretty enough for Gerald. For anyone. What makes a face pretty anyway?

yes, pretty?

No, not pretty?

I read that scientists have actually studied this, and what we consider beautiful is really symmetry. So, is my face symmetrical? My eyes too small? my nose too big?

I can't tell. It's just my face, the same one I've always had except not as round as when I was little. And more pimply (though not too much — I've seen way worse).

After Art was P.E., always horrible, but at least today was just a rules day. We didn't actually do anything except stare at the clock, waiting for the final bell to ring.

BRRRRRRNNGGG!

And then it was over, my first day as an 8th grader. Carly and I walked home together and compared notes on P.E. teachers. She has Mr. Takahashi and I have Ms. Pollard.

Then she started talking about Gerald again. That girl doesn't know when to stop!

"Are you going to tell him you like him?" she asked. "Want me to ask around and find out if he likes you?"

"Are you crazy?!" Of course I wasn't going to say ANYTHING to Gerald and no way did I want Carly to ask about me. What could be more embarrassing?

"So you're just going to pine after him in silence?" she pushed.

"Carly, please! Just leave me alone!" She thought I was being touchy and maybe I was, but I'm so not good at the boy thing. She said I need to have more confidence, believe in myself. Easy for her to say. Boys are a complete mystery to me. Maybe if I had a brother, things would be different, but I don't.

Lucky Carly has two great older brothers.

All I get is Cleo.

Anatomy of a Boy?

↓

what do they think about? Video games, sports, fixing things? Or do they think of the same things girls do — friends, enemies, frenemies?

→

Adam's apple — what is this for and why do boys have it? To make their voices tougher, stronger, lower, louder?

←

What do they like to do? What's their idea of fun? Drinking a soda so fast it foams out their nose? Having burping contests? Playing laser tag? I have NO idea!

←

What makes a girl interesting to them? Her jokes? Her face? Her → body? How she dresses? if she can sing or run or play basketball?

I couldn't talk to Carly about this, but
I could write to Nadia, my old best friend.
She'd understand because, like me, she's
not cool.

I've known Nadia
practically
my whole
life.
→

She's smart
and sweet, but
doesn't have
that undefinable
something
that
makes
you cool!
↙

I could e-mail or IM her, but usually
when I write to Nadia, I do it the old-
fashioned way and that's how she writes
back to me. There's something special
about getting mail you can hold in your
hands. It's definitely worth the wait.
In fact, waiting is part of what makes
it mean more.

And for me, writing stuff down helps
me figure out what I'm feeling.

I know most kids text, but Mom says I can't have a cell phone until I can pay for it myself. Which is the same thing she says about getting my ears pierced. Which is basically like saying never.

At least I can write — whenever and whatever I want! Plus there's nothing like pen on paper. Low tech maybe, but high magic.

Anyway here's what I wrote to Nadia.

↓

Dear Nadia,
Happy 8th Grade! How do you like it so far? For me the best part is — believe it or not — a boy, Gerald. He's super-cute and sits next to me in Science (only it wasn't his choice, the teacher assigned seats). He's also in English/Social Studies, so we have three periods together. Do you have any ideas how I can make him like me? Yours till the boy scouts, amelia

Nadia Kurz
61 South St.
Barton, CA
91010

The good thing about writing to Nadia (besides the fact that she gives useful advice) is that once I put things down on paper, it's out of my head so I don't worry about it as much. Usually that's what happens. This time I couldn't stop thinking about Gerald no matter what. Was there ANYTHING I could do to make him see me differently tomorrow? Anything that could make me pretty?

I scrounged through my closet, searching for something, anything, that would transform me into a cool girl.

All I found were embarrassing monstrosities like bright orange — ORANGE! — sweaters and plaid vests. Who wears vests? Who wears Plaid? Or orange anything (except for road work crews)? How did these horrors get in my closet?

"Whadya doin' there?" Cleo asked, poking her famous jelly roll nose where it didn't belong.

Looking for a Halloween costume? Kinda early, isn't it?

"Go away!" I wasn't in the mood to deal with Cleo.

"Don't get all huffy. How do you like 8th grade? Do you have Mrs. Kiljerky for English? She's hilarious! My theory is that with a name like hers, she had to develop a good sense of humor. It was a survival mechanism."

"No," I snapped. "I have Mr. Hoyle. A teacher with a normal name and probably NO sense of humor."

"You really are in a mood," Cleo said, still standing in my doorway, still staring at my ugly clothes.

"Can you just go away?" I begged.

"Don't you want some sisterly advice? After all, I'm older than you. I'm a sophomore in high school now. And with my superior experience and wisdom, I can tell you right now — get rid of those clothes!"

I sat on the floor, surrounded by bad taste, my bad taste.

She was right. How had I ever worn any of it?

"Why didn't you tell me before? How could you let me wear such awful stuff?"

"As if you'd listen to me!"

She was right. I wouldn't have. I stared at Cleo, trying to see her as if she was a stranger.

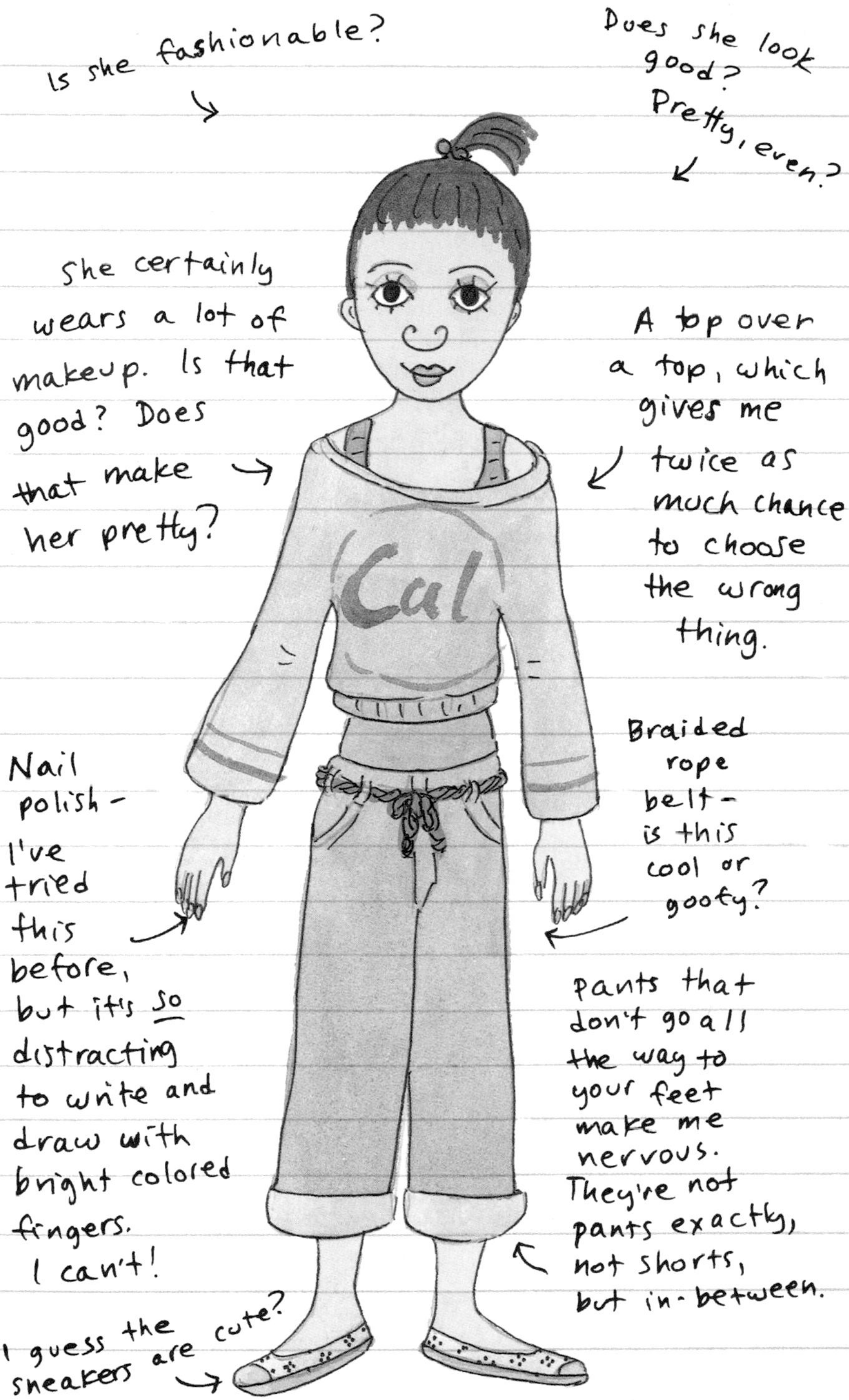
Is she fashionable?
Does she look good? Pretty, even?
She certainly wears a lot of makeup. Is that good? Does that make her pretty?
A top over a top, which gives me twice as much chance to choose the wrong thing.
Cal
Nail polish - I've tried this before, but it's so distracting to write and draw with bright colored fingers. I can't!
Braided rope belt - is this cool or goofy?
pants that don't go all the way to your feet make me nervous. They're not pants exactly, not shorts, but in-between.
I guess the sneakers are cute?

It was nice of Cleo to offer her help, really it was. Except help from her might be more like sabotage. She might make me even uglier. I couldn't risk it.

"I can help you with makeup, too," Cleo said.

That was it. NO! She knew how I felt about makeup.

"You're older now," she said. "You're allowed to change your mind."

"I haven't," I said. "Not yet." But once the idea was planted, I couldn't get it out of my head.

maybe a little makeup, just a little, would make Gerald like me.

Would I be prettier this way? If only Mom would let me pierce my ears!

"Suit yourself." Cleo shrugged and left me alone with a pile of the ugliest, saddest clothes ever. There wasn't a single thing I could wear as an 8th grader. I didn't want to borrow stuff from Cleo (who's way bigger than me anyway), and I know what Mom would say if I asked for new clothes.

Money doesn't grow on trees.

You have plenty of clothes that fit and aren't worn out.

wear those.

Mom's one of those grown-ups who don't remember anything of what it's like to be a kid. Otherwise she would know that fitting and not having holes are totally beside the point. When I was little it didn't matter so much that I wore lumpy, frumpy things. Now it does!

Why don't they teach us what makes good clothes, good style instead of decimals and fractions? What's more important, knowing the capital of Delaware or how to dress for success?

If I was the principal, these are the classes I would give to the 8th graders:

Clothes 101: What to wear, what to burn.

Foreign Language: How to talk to boys — in English and French.

History: How to make your past sound fascinating and create the future you dream of.

English: How to be a brilliant speaker, write amazing stories. Plus read lots of great books!

Science: How to understand the male brain and heart. Plus potions, experiments, and explosions — all cool!

Now I'm sounding ridiculously boy crazy when I'm not! I'm only interested in one boy right now, and that's Gerald. And it's not like I'm obsessive or anything. I just want him to like me. That's perfectly normal for an 8th grader!

Anyway, there's no way to read Gerald's mind or figure out the Male Brain, but I can work on the clothes thing. And the person to talk to about that was Carly.

Hey, Carly, I thought I'd get some clothes ideas from you.

Your mom's letting you buy new things?

Um, I haven't asked her yet. But if she says yes, what should I get?

We have to go shopping. You have to try things on, see what's cute on you.

That's the problem. Nothing is cute on me.

We made a plan to go shopping next weekend even though I bet Mom won't let me. I've got to earn money so I can buy what I want. Carly and I should start babysitting again. We didn't make a lot of money, but it was something.

I looked in my piggy bank. →

I had $33.17. What could I get with that? Shirt? Shoes. One maybe?

↑
It was hopeless!

I'm not in high school yet and already everything is so complicated. How does Cleo do it? She always has a boyfriend, a steady stream of loud, oily, gangly guys.

↑
Not my types at all, but they clearly like Cleo so I have to give her some credit. She probably knows how boys' brains work or something, not that I would EVER ask her!

For days, I tried EVERYTHING to get Gerald to like me. I brought in cookies for the entire class and made sure he got two when everyone else got one. I laughed whenever he said anything the slightest, tiniest bit funny. I smiled so much my face felt stiff.

All I could think about was Gerald, Gerald, GERALD. Did he notice me at all?

Carly said I was trying too hard. I told her I wasn't doing anything special, but she's too smart to believe that.

The cookies were a sure tip-off. The last time I brought in a treat without a class party or a birthday was for the school bake-off when EVERYONE brought in baked goods. No wonder Carly smelled a rat — a chocolaty rat, but still a rat.

So at lunch that day, on Thursday at 12:11 pm, I told the truth. I admitted that I like Gerald. "Like" liked, that way.

"I knew it! What kind of friend would I be if I couldn't tell? So _he's_ the reason we're going shopping this weekend? He's why you're trying so hard to be a completely different person?"

"I'm not trying to be different, just better. More likeable." I slumped down in my seat. "It's exhausting. And no matter what I do, I can't tell if it's working or not. I keep hinting about the dance — which is <u>tomorrow</u> by the way — and he still hasn't asked me. What do I have to do, ask him myself?"

"Why don't you?"

"Ask him?! Are you crazy?" I couldn't believe Carly! I have a rule — don't ask if you don't want to hear a "no." It works with my mom or when I want to "borrow" Cleo's music.

I don't want to hear Gerald say "no." I'd <u>never</u> recover!

"Why not? Where is it written that girls have to wait for boys to ask?" Carly, naturally, has her own rules.

"It's not written because EVERYONE knows that's just the way it is." Especially me, I know that.

"So change it. You can be the first girl brave enough to ask a boy to the dance!'"

That's hardly a dramatic first for girls, like the first woman to fly an airplane, the first woman elected to Congress, the first woman to win a Nobel Peace Prize. (Has a woman done that?)

First woman astronaut in the U.S.A., Sally Ride. The first woman in space was a Russian.

Sandra Day o'Connor

First woman on the Supreme Court.

First woman to conduct a major symphony orchestra.

Nadia Boulanger

In fact, I bet there are already girls who've asked boys out and they had a much better chance of getting a "yes" than I do. So I wouldn't be the first. Still, Carly had a point. Why do I have to wait for him to see that I'm perfect for him?

"What if he says no?" I asked.

Carly shrugged. "Then you'll know what it's like for a guy to ask a girl. Anyway, what's so terrible if he does turn you down? Is that worse than him _not_ asking you?"

"Yes! It's way worse! One's a big, fat nothing. The other is a big, fat rejection."

I thought of all the ways rejection hurts. It's not a pretty picture.

↑
not getting any valentines

↑
not being invited to a birthday party

not being picked for a baseball team — or being picked last

not being included in a game ↳

not winning an art contest

But sad though all that was, I couldn't shake what Carly had said. At least I'd be doing something, and that felt better, stronger, than waiting. And even though I'm sure I wouldn't be the first girl ever to ask a boy to a dance, it still felt risky and adventurous and exciting. Scary, even. I had to try!

I saw my chance at the end of lunch. I told Carly to watch me, I was going to do it.

I walked right up to Gerald.

Hey, Amelia!

Um, hey!

I don't know what happened! I couldn't say anything. It was all because he said something first. That threw me off!

"Nice one, Amelia," Carly said.

"I'll try again. Today." I meant it. I just had to make sure I talked first, before Gerald could make me nervous.

I looked for him in the halls between classes, but I didn't get another chance until right before Science.

My hands were sweaty. My mouth was dry. My stomach was churning. It was now or never. I didn't think. I just opened my mouth and let the words tumble out.

Want to go to the dance with me tomorrow?

← squeaky, raspy voice

He stared at me. I froze. I couldn't repeat those words, I just couldn't. So I stood there, waiting, a simpering smile plastered on my face. I hated who I was at that minute.

And maybe he felt the same way because after an eternity he said, "The dance? With you?" He turned away as if he couldn't face me, and I already knew the answer. "Um, no, I'm really sorry."

"Uh, okay," I mumbled, embarrassment flooding my face. Even my ears must have turned red. Why did I ask him BEFORE class? Now I had to sit next to him feeling the waves of awkwardness radiating between us. I didn't hear a word the teacher said. All I heard was "Loser, loser, loser" echoing in my brain.

I just wanted to sink into the floor. ↙

At least I was so miserable, even Sadie couldn't make me feel worse. I knew she was giving me her → usual evil eye, but I didn't care.

I told Carly what happened on the way home after school.

"How will I ever show my face again?! It was SO embarrassing!"

Carly thought I was overreacting. "It's his loss. He may be cute, but he's not the right boy for you."

"How do you know?"

"Because he didn't say yes."

Maybe that was my fault. Maybe I came on too strong. Maybe I startled him so he blurted out "no" since that was safer than "yes." Or maybe Carly was right. It was all such a muddle.

So I did what I usually do when I'm trying to figure things out. I wrote a story.

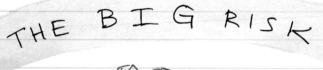

THE BIG RISK

Roll the dice — take a chance!

There was a girl who was a daring, intrepid explorer. She'd climbed Mt. Everest, rafted down the Amazon river, snowshoed across Antarctica. She was good at tying knots, forging trails, and camping in the wilderness.

which would you rather face – a cute boy or a tarantula? →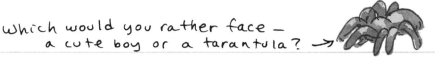

But she had no idea how to talk to boys. They were scarier to her than giant pythons or poisonous scorpions.

She was back from one of her explorations when she saw a sign advertising "A Night of Music and Memories." It was a dance. The girl had done a lot of things, but she'd never gone to a dance. She'd never had a night of music and memories.

She decided it was time she tried one. → A dance, that is.

She even knew a boy she liked, a fellow explorer who she could ask to come ← with her. Or could she?

She had faced charging rhinos, thundering avalanches, and angry elephants, but that simple phone call terrified her. Don't be silly, she told herself and dialed the number.

Before she could change her mind, she blurted out her question. "Will you go to a dance with me?"

"Who is this?" the boy asked.

She almost hung up. She almost lied. But she didn't. She took a deep breath and said her name.

"Why, yes!" he said. "That would be delightful!"

And it was.

That's one ending. Here's another:

"I'm sorry!" he huffed. "I should do the asking. If you do it, that's pushy, bossy even. Not at all ladylike."

"No," she snapped. "It isn't. But then neither is exploring and having adventures."

"Now that you mention it, those aren't things girls should do. You should probably stop."

"I don't think so, but I should definitely stop talking to you!" She thought she'd feel hurt or sad, but all she felt was mad. So she started packing for her next adventure and immediately felt much better.

bug spray
↓

sleeping bag
↓

unladylike luggage
↙

← machete

That made me feel better. And clearer. I could even face seeing Gerald again so long as I NEVER talked to him again.

The next day in English/Social Studies was better than I thought it would be. I had Carly with me and we didn't sit anywhere near Gerald. I could almost pretend he didn't exist. But what would happen in Science when I had to sit next to him?

Now at lunch I wasn't obsessing about how to get Gerald to like me, but how to make sure he didn't notice me.

I wished I had a cloak of invisibility. That would be handy!

"How are you doing?" Carly asked.

"Okay, I guess. I think I'm over Gerald. Except now he probably hates me, so on one side I have him and on the other, there's Sadie."

Talk about being between a rock and a hard place!

"Who cares about Sadie? She's old history."
Just as Carly said that, who should walk by but Sadie. I didn't say anything. Neither did Carly. And Sadie didn't, either. Maybe she was bored with being mad at me. Now she could just ignore me — I hoped. Then I'd be between a rock and an icicle, not too bad.

But try as she could, Sadie couldn't ignore me. She whipped around and snarled at me.

I know what you're doing! You think he likes you? He has WAY better taste than that! Guess who's going to the dance with Gerald?

ME! That's who! HAH!

I was so shocked, I didn't know what to say.

I felt like a fish blowing bubbles out of its mouth. Blurp, blurp, blurp!

Right then I didn't care about Gerald. I was too afraid of Sadie. I'm not proud to admit it, but it's true.

I held up my hands like I was surrendering. I guess I was.

Okay, Sadie, you're right.

You win!

Good for you. I'm happy for you, really.

She had been all puffed up with triumph and rage, but now she looked like an old, deflated balloon.

"Really? You're happy for me? You're not teasing me?"

"No, Sadie, really." And at that moment, I meant it. I wanted something to make her feel better, to take the edge off her anger. I definitely didn't care about Gerald. Well, hardly at all. Most of all, I wanted her to stop yelling at me.

"Okay, then." A pale smile twitched across her face. "No hard feelings."

Now it was my turn to be relieved. "So you're done with being mad at me? Really, truly done?"

She nodded and walked away.

Carly and I gaped at each other.

"Who knew?" Carly asked. "Could you tell she liked Gerald? Could you tell he liked her?"

I shook my head. "I was too busy trying to make him like me, I guess." I felt pretty stupid. Was I really that oblivious?

"I'm really sorry. I wish I'd noticed."

"Me, too," I said. "But maybe you're right, it's for the best. He's not the right boy for me if she's the kind of girl he likes. No way I can be at all like Sadie!"

Besides being tall and blond while I'm short and dark, Sadie's a constant talker. →

She asks zillions of questions, is super-gushy about everything, unless she's mad at you. Then she's just plain scary. ↙

I don't want her for a friend. And I really don't want her for an enemy. ↗

I don't want to be even a tiny bit like her. Even if that means no Gerald for a boyfriend. ←

Carly agreed. "You're nothing like Sadie! Good thing, too, because when she likes you, she's too close. When she hates you, she's still too close."

"She's perfect this way," I said. "Just leaving me alone."

I had Science after lunch, my one class with Sadie AND Gerald. I started to sit in my seat, but then I got an idea.

"Hey," I whispered to Sadie. "Want to trade? He's your boyfriend, after all."

She turned bright pink. She looked happy, really happy, as she sat next to the boy I'd been studying for the past few days. He was still cute, but not in the same way, not now that I knew about him and Sadie.

Gerald mooning over Sadie.
↓

Sadie mooning over Gerald.
↓

me, wondering if anyone will ever moon over me that way.
↙

When class was over, Sadie waited for me by the door.

"Thanks, Amelia. That was really nice of you. Even though we're <u>not</u> friends."

"I'm just glad we're not enemies." Which was true. I don't want another messy friendship with Sadie <u>at all</u>.

I guess I'm okay at figuring out other girls. But boys are another story. I couldn't get Gerald to like me, but I could make him <u>not</u> like me. I guess the moral of the story is that boys <u>are</u> like girls in some ways. You can't make ANYONE like you, not really. Either they do or they don't. And if you act all fake to make a friend, then they're not a true friend anyway.

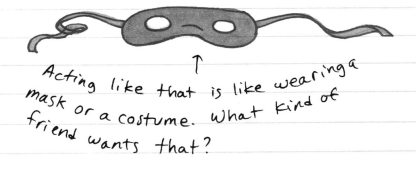

↑
Acting like that is like wearing a mask or a costume. What kind of friend wants that?

When I got home from school, there was a postcard from Nadia, now that it was too late.

Dear Amelia,

Funny that you wrote to me about a boy, because guess what? George asked me to the 8th grade dance! I didn't do anything — he just asked. All I can say is be yourself because don't you want to be liked for who you really are? That's something we learned in kindergarten, remember?

Amelia
564 North Homecrest
Oopa, Oregon
97881

Yours till the friend ships, Nadia

A boy asked Nadia to the dance?! I guess that proves you don't have to be super-cool for a boy to like you. That gives me hope! And she's right, of course, about being true to yourself. That's just what I was writing about with the mask and acting and stuff like that.

I didn't go to the dance that night. And I didn't go clothes shopping that weekend, either.

Instead I played basketball with Carly and her brothers. Maybe if I spend time with boys as regular friends, it won't be so hard to understand them. It's worth the experiment, especially since Malcolm and Marcus are a lot of fun. And cute, very cute, much more cute than Gerald.

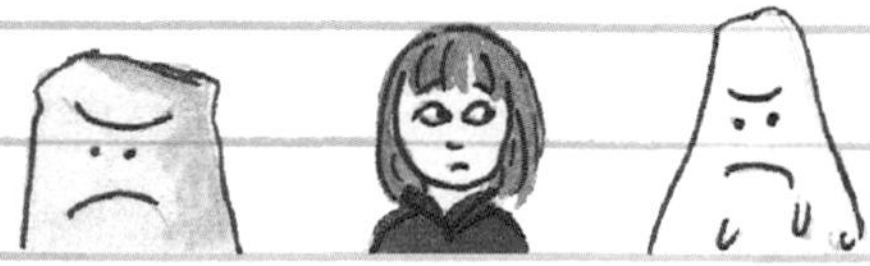

MORE Amelia's Notebooks

write on! ↓

I've written ~~22~~ ~~23~~ notebooks! which is your favorite?

Read on! ↓

The good, the bad, and the totally freaky! ↓

I wish I could forget them! ↑

← Pssst! Did you hear the one about Mr. L?

Amelia's 6th-Grade Notebook

Amelia's MOST UNFORGETTABLE EMBARRASSING MOMENTS

Amelia's BOX OF NOTES for NOTE PASSING

Amelia's LONGEST BIGGEST MOST-FIGHTS-EVER FAMILY REUNION

Amelia's GUIDE to GOSSIP

Amelia's MIDDLE SCHOOL SURVIVAL GUIDE

VOTE 4 Amelia

Amelia's Itchy-Twitchy, Lovey-Dovey Summer CAMP MOSQUITO

Amelia's GUIDE TO BABYSITTING

Amelia's SCIENCE FAIR DISASTER

Amelia's 7th-Grade Notebook

↑ Carly's favorite so far!

Plus all these from elementary school ↓

The first and original! →

Amelia's Notebook

Amelia's Bully Survival Guide

Amelia's Boredom Survival Guide

CAUTION Amelia Writes Again CAUTION

Amelia's School Survival Guide

↑ Still my favorite!

Amelia's 5th-Grade Notebook

Amelia's Most-Keep RESOLUTIONS for the BEST YEAR EVER

The All-New Amelia

Amelia's Family Ties

Amelia Tells All

There's lots more info and fun stuff at marissamoss.com and KIDS.simonandschuster.com. Even a real Amelia movie!